Cat Tales

The Cat Who Wasn't There

Cat Tales

The Cat Who Wasn't There

LINDA NEWBERY

Illustrated by Stephen Lambert

USBORNE

For Peter and Saira, with love,
and thanks for the title.

First published in the UK in 2009 by Usborne Publishing Ltd.,
Usborne House, 83-85 Saffron Hill, London EC1N 8RT, England.
www.usborne.com

Text copyright © Linda Newbery, 2009

Illustration copyright © Usborne Publishing Ltd., 2009

A CIP catalogue record for this book is available from the British Library.

JFMAMJJ SOND/09 92241   ISBN 9780746097328 Printed in Great Britain.

Chapter One

If you asked Vincent if he was happy, he'd have to think about it for a moment. Then he'd say yes, he supposed he was.

No one *did* ask, though. It wasn't the sort of question anyone thought of. Not even Vincent himself. To anyone else who knew him, he seemed to be exactly the same from one year to the next.

There was nothing, really, to make him *un*happy. He had everything he needed. He lived in the same small house he'd lived in for years. He had friends. He had a little garden to sit in on warm days.

Most of all, he had his paintings. At the end of the garden was his painting shed, and there he kept his easel and his paints, his pencils and his crayons. It was warm in winter, cool in summer. Hours and hours he spent there, mixing and thinking, flicking and dabbing.

Every December, Vincent's art club
held a special exhibition at the town
hall. Vincent always had half a wall to
himself, with ten or twelve or fifteen of
his paintings on show. They were for
sale, and most of them would be
bought. Sometimes, if he'd painted
something very special, he put a blue
sticker on its frame, which meant NOT
FOR SALE.

Of course, that would be the painting everyone wanted. That was the way it went.

Vincent painted all year round, but from summer onwards he was thinking about the art club show. He painted and painted and painted. Every morning he went down to his shed, turned on the radio and hummed to himself while he mixed his colours. After a while, he'd stand back and squint at his easel, and know that he was painting well.

He could paint lots of things – but the one thing he just couldn't do was people. Any people he drew looked like untidy bunches of sticks. He'd tried and tried, but could never get any better. So he didn't put people in his pictures at all.

He painted woods, beaches, parks, houses, gardens and empty streets.

This year, though, he wasn't happy. Each day he started a new painting, but he knew it wouldn't turn out well. He stood back and stared; he tutted and he frowned and he scowled. He mixed new

colours; he swished and he dabbed, he worked and worked and worked and then gazed at what he'd done.

Always, till now, his paintings had been admired. "You could almost walk across that grass," someone would say, or, "I can smell the roses!" or, "That lake looks wet enough to swim in."

This new lot of pictures, though...

They were flat. Dull. No breath of life in them. Something was missing, and it was the most important thing of all.

Day after day Vincent worked. He made himself finish the pictures. But he didn't like a single one of them.

He stared and stared, trying to work out what was wrong. He mixed more paint, and had another go at the picture on his easel. He squidged and he smudged and he scraped, but only made more of a mess.

"I'm losing it, that's what," he said to himself. "Too old, that's my trouble. Might as well give up."

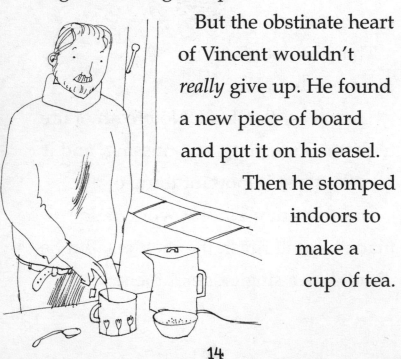

But the obstinate heart of Vincent wouldn't *really* give up. He found a new piece of board and put it on his easel.

Then he stomped indoors to make a cup of tea.

To cheer himself up, he opened a packet of biscuits.

As he walked along the garden path, back to his shed, something caught his eye.

Something white.

Something slinky.

Chapter Two

It was a small white cat, lifting its paws carefully over the damp grass. It paused. Bright eyes looked straight at Vincent.

For a moment he could hardly breathe. Then he whispered, "Snow?"

The cat's mouth opened in a silent miaow. It stepped towards him. Stiffly,

Vincent bent, holding out a hand in welcome. The cat butted him, and a purr spread warmly through its body.

"Snow, Snow!" said Vincent, almost in a sob. "My good old friend! You've come back!"

He gathered the cat in his arms, and breathed the clean smell of its fur. He felt choked with joy. *This* was what had been missing.

The cat struggled free and jumped down; but it didn't run away.

It stalked round the garden, tail high.
Then it dashed and pounced at a scatter
of leaves, and rolled over, clutching one
dried leaf between
its front paws.

Vincent laughed. "Silly old Snow! Daft
as ever! Where've you been all this time?
You must be hungry. Don't go away."
And he kept glancing back at the cat as
he went into his kitchen and opened the

fridge to see what he could find. Yes, there were some pieces of cooked chicken left over from last night's dinner.

One odd thing was that the cat was wearing a blue collar. Vincent puzzled over that as he put a small piece of chicken on a saucer. Hadn't Snow's collar been purple? Maybe it had faded, after so long.

He carried the saucer out to his painting shed. "Snow, Snow! Come on, Snow!" he called softly, and the cat gave a little chirrup, and trotted after him. It ate the chicken hungrily, then looked up at Vincent and miaowed.

"Here's your chair, and your cushion, see?" Vincent told it. In one corner of the shed stood a wooden chair with a soft green cushion on its seat. There was a cat-sized dent where Snow used to sleep, and some of his white hairs made a soft lining. Vincent patted the cushion.

The cat was keen on exploring the shed, and didn't want to sit. It swiped at the top of a paint tube, then found a piece of string and chased that. Vincent watched for a while, smiling. Then he thought he'd better walk to the shops to buy cat food.

"You won't go away again, Snow, will you?" he said to the cat. "You're here to stay now."

As he went indoors for his coat and his cap, his money and his shopping bag, his heart was full of happiness.

Out in the street, Vincent saw Tom and Tabitha Pringle, the two children who lived opposite.

"Skitter!" they were shouting. "Skitty!"

He supposed it must be some kind of game. They were nice children and Vincent always said hello to them, and to their mother, Maggie.

"Hello!" he called now.

"We're looking for our new cat," Tom called back. "Have you seen her? She's little and white. And she's got a blue collar."

Vincent felt dizzy.

Of course. Of course the cat in his garden wasn't Snow.

How could it be?

Snow had died a year ago. He was buried at the end of the garden, under the apple tree.

Chapter Three

I don't know what's the matter with me!
Vincent thought. *Playing a trick on myself
like that – such a silly trick!*

But he made his voice cheerful,
especially when he saw that Tabby was
crying. "Don't you worry!" he told the
children. "Your little cat's in my back

garden. I didn't know it was yours."

"Oh!" went Tabby, and gave him a big, teary smile.

"I'll tell Mum," said Tom. "She's knocking at all the doors."

A few minutes later, all three Pringles – the children and their mother, Maggie – were standing in Vincent's garden, calling the cat, who was now high in the apple tree.

"Skitty!"

"Skittercat!"

"Skitzy! How're you going to get *down*?"

The cat stared, miaowed, and started to come down the tree.

"She seems to have a lot of names," said Vincent.

"Skitter, that's her proper name," said Maggie. "She's a kitten-cat, six months old. We've only had her two weeks, and this is just her second time out, so she's exploring. I'm sorry she bothered you."

"Oh, no, no!" Vincent protested. "No bother at all! I love cats. In fact I used to have one just like her. Snow, he was called."

"What happened to him?" asked Tom.

"He got old and ill. I had to have him put to sleep," Vincent explained, and Tabby looked sad all over again. As Skitter reached the ground, Tabby ran to her and picked her up in a big cuddle. "Here's Snow's place," said Vincent, showing the little grave at the foot of the tree, marked by a large grey stone with SNOW and a scatter of snowflakes painted on it. "He used to like sitting up in the tree, so this is where he's buried."

They all looked, but now Tom was

more interested in the shed. Maggie
turned to look too.

"Oh! How lovely! And are those your
paintings inside?"

"Are you a real artist?" said Tabby,
big-eyed, still cuddling Skitter.

"Maybe, yes, sometimes." Vincent was

embarrassed. "But not a very good one."

Tom was already in the doorway.
"They look good to me!"

"Tom!" Maggie tugged him back by

his sweatshirt. "Vincent hasn't said you can go in."

"That's all right, Tom. You're welcome to have a look," said Vincent.

To distract attention from his awful paintings, he showed them Snow's chair. "Look, he used to sit here while I painted. Kept me company. See, that's the dent he made in the cushion, and his white hairs. I haven't had the heart to brush them off, because that'd be the very last of him gone."

Maggie looked sorry. "You must miss him very badly."

"Yes," said Vincent. "I do."

After the Pringles had gone, taking Skitter with them, Vincent sat in Snow's chair, not caring about white hairs on his trousers. Yes, he did miss Snow very badly indeed. Snow had been his friend, his companion. The shed seemed empty

without him.

Even though he'd known, really, that Snow couldn't possibly have come back, Vincent felt so heavy with disappointment that he went to bed early. He didn't read late into the night, as he usually did. He turned off his lamp and lay in the darkness, thinking about Snow.

So perhaps it wasn't surprising that, when he fell asleep, he *dreamed* about Snow.

Chapter Four

In his dream, Vincent was trying to
paint, and doing very badly indeed. He
could hardly lift the brush, and when he
did, it made a great brown splodge,
which he tried to turn into a tree. Paint
sploshed everywhere except where he
wanted it. His hands might have been

bunches of bananas, for all the use they were.

Turning away in disgust, he looked out of the window. He hadn't noticed that it was snowing, but now big flakes were falling: spinning, whirling, making him dizzy. And there, through them, across the garden, was Snow.

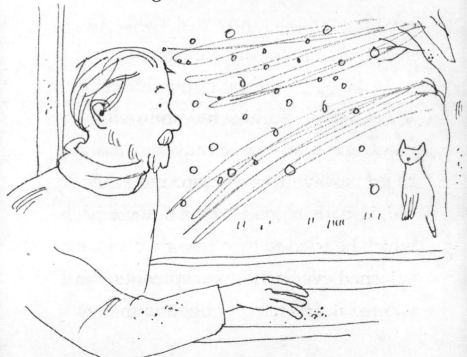

"Snow!" Vincent tried to call, but his voice came out as a croak. "Snow! Where've you *been* all this time?"

Snow heard the feeble calling, and stepped across the cold grass, lifting his paws. He was as white and sleek as Vincent remembered, and his eyes were as bright.

With a bound, Snow was inside the shed, purring like an engine. He jumped up to his chair and settled himself on his cushion, looking around as if he'd never been away.

Vincent's heart filled with joy.

He grabbed a new piece of board,
mixed fresh colours and began again.
The paint flowed from his brush. The
picture sprang into bright, gleaming
life. He was happy.

Then, slowly, he woke up to his quiet
bedroom and the ticking of the clock,
and he knew that it was just a dream.
Snow hadn't
really come
back. And
never would.

All day, Vincent felt so dreary that he didn't even try to paint. Instead, he made himself do some washing and ironing. The day passed very, very slowly. But, just as it was starting to get dark, the doorbell rang. It was Maggie Pringle, with Tabby.

"Hello?" said Vincent, trying to make a smiley face.

Maggie looked awkward. "We were just wondering...the thing is, we're going to visit my sister at the weekend, and we were going to put Skitter in the cattery. But then we thought – well, you seem to like cats, and you seem to like Skitter – do you think you might look after her for us?"

Now Vincent's smile was real. "Yes, I'd like that! Thank you!"

Maggie and Tabby thanked him five times each, and then they all went across to the Pringles' house so that Vincent could be given a key and shown what to do. Skitter would have to stay indoors, Maggie explained; otherwise she might wander off again. Vincent promised to come three times each day: morning and evening to feed Skitter, and at lunchtime just to check, or to play games.

Tabby looked as if she wanted to say something, and at last she did. "If you like cats so much, why don't you get another one?" she asked Vincent. "We got Skitter from the RSPCA. They've got lots of nice cats that want homes."

"It's a kind thought, Tabby," said Vincent, shaking his head. "But I just couldn't. Another cat wouldn't be the same as Snow."

Still, he went home feeling very
pleased that he was being trusted with
Skitter, and doing something useful.

The Pringles left on Friday afternoon.
That evening, Vincent let himself in with

his key, fed Skitter, played ball-chase up
and down the stairs, and cleaned the
litter tray.

On Saturday morning, though, things
went badly wrong.

Chapter Five

It was a cold, cold morning, and as Vincent walked up the Pringles' front path and turned his key in the lock, he was wishing he'd put on his coat.

Skitter must have been waiting for her chance. Hardly had Vincent pushed the door open than there was a brush of

fur against his legs, and a white
streaking rush. Skitter was out!

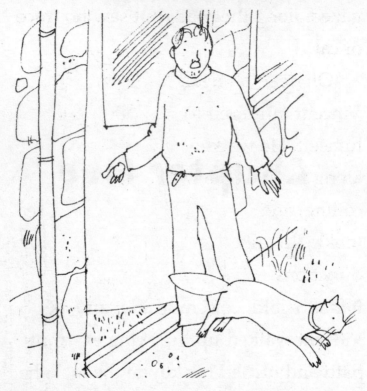

"Skitter! Come back!" Vincent
shouted, in a panic. "Breakfast!"
She'd hurtled off at such speed that
he couldn't see where she'd gone. He

closed the door, and looked in next door's front garden, then the next. He gazed along the road, but saw no trace of cat.

"Oh dear, oh dear," Vincent muttered to himself. He walked along the pavement, calling, and looking in all directions. Not a hair or a whisker of Skitter could he see.

What if something awful happened? What if Skitter got lost, or even got *run over*?

The Pringles would never forgive him. He'd never forgive *himself*. He felt quite shaky and dithery. His eyes had gone blurry, seeking and seeking a white cat shape. How could he explain to Tabby that her cat was lost again? What would he *say*?

No sign of Skitter! She must have gone round behind the houses, into one of the back gardens. There was nothing for it but to knock on all the doors along the street until he found her.

He knocked at the house next to the Pringles', but no one was in.

He rang the doorbell of Mrs. Crossley's house, the next one along, but she said that her dog would growl if a cat came into the garden.

The third house along had its front
door open, because Lisa and Ben who
lived there had just driven up in their
car, and were carrying their bags of
shopping inside. They checked their
back garden, and promised to let
Vincent know if Skitter turned up.

All down that side of the street
Vincent went, knocking and ringing,
waiting and explaining. He went
beyond the point where he knew the
neighbours' names. When he reached
the end of the road, he worked his way
back on his own side.

"Little white cat? No,
haven't seen it."

"I *did* see a cat, but that
one was
black and white."

"What, that one that was
lost the other day? Lost
again, is it?
No, sorry. Can't help you."

Vincent began to feel
quite desperate. He was

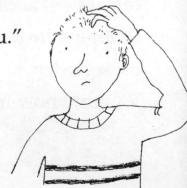

shivering with cold and panic. What if…
what if…? No, he must stop thinking
about *what ifs*, and concentrate on
finding Skitter. She couldn't be far
away!

Four doors from his own, the
Lawrence family had moved out, and
someone new had moved in. Vincent
had seen the removal van two days ago,
when he walked past on his way to the
shops.

He rang the doorbell, and when
someone answered he asked, for the
fourteenth time: "Sorry to bother you,
but have you seen a little
white cat, with a blue
collar?"

"Yes," said the woman

who stood there. "As a matter of fact I have. It's in my garden now. Is it yours?"

Vincent felt dizzy with relief. His head swam, and he almost toppled over.

The woman looked anxious. "Oh dear, you don't look well at all! Blue with cold! Come on in and sit down for a moment. It's a chilly day to be out with no coat on."

She looked down at Vincent's feet, and he realized that he was wearing his slippers. He'd only meant to go across the road and back. What must he look like?

He was too dazed to answer, but the woman looked at him kindly and said,

"Let me make you a nice cup of tea! We're neighbours, aren't we? So we might as well be friends. My name's Jeannie."

"Skitter," croaked Vincent.

"Well, Mr. Skitter, come and sit down by the fire—"

"No! No, I'm Vincent. Skitter's the cat. I must catch her first."

"Don't you worry about her," said Jeannie, who seemed the kind of person who made everything easy. She led the way indoors to a room warmed by a gas fire; then she opened French windows that led to the garden and called, "Skitter!" And at once Skitter came bounding in. Jeannie found a ball of wool, and soon Skitter was happily chasing it round the chair legs.

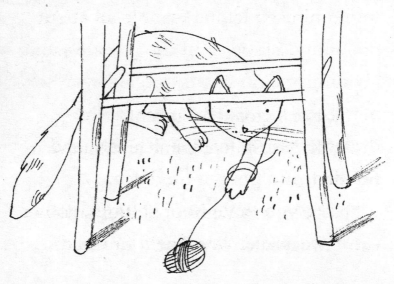

At last, Vincent could smile and relax. It was nice to sit here in the warmth, with someone friendly to talk to. Jeannie's own cat, Boris, sat on the rug, opening one eye now and then. He didn't seem to mind being visited by a boisterous kitten-cat, except for once when Skitter crashed into him; then he gave a lazy swipe with a front paw.

Over tea and buttered toast, Vincent found himself telling Jeannie all about Snow, and Skitter, and the Pringles, and about his painting failures. He even told her about the dream he'd had, the dream of Snow. Jeannie listened, and nodded, and poured more tea.

"Have you thought of getting another cat?" she asked, when he'd finished.

"People say I should," said Vincent. "But it just wouldn't seem right."

Jeannie thought for a moment.

"Perhaps," she said, "what you should do is *paint* cats."

Chapter Six

For the rest of the weekend, Vincent looked after Skitter without letting her out again.

Jeannie came round on Sunday to see how he was, and he showed her the paintings in his shed, even the awful ones. At once she found one she liked,

a mountain scene that Vincent had
painted on holiday in Wales. She
wanted to buy it, but Vincent said he
wouldn't take money.

"Please, let me give it to you! You've been so kind."

"No, no – that's very sweet of you," said Jeannie, "but I insist on paying!"

"No, no," said Vincent, who could be just as obstinate, "I insist that you don't."

Jeannie was first to give in. "In that case, you must let me invite you for lunch one day next week. Then you can see your painting on my wall, and tell me how you're getting on with the cat pictures."

The Pringles came home that evening, and were very pleased to see Skitter. They gave Vincent a pot plant as a present. He protested that he didn't deserve it, for letting Skitter escape; but

Maggie said that Skitter was as slippery
as an eel, and the point was he'd *found*
her again.

Next morning Vincent felt full of
purpose. He took the pot plant out to
his painting shed. Then he tidied

everything. He cleaned his
brushes and washed his
jars, arranged his
tubes of paint,
and stacked the
worst of his pictures
where he didn't
have to look at them.

Now he was ready to start.

This shouldn't be too difficult! He
knew cats. He knew how they moved,
and how they behaved. He knew how
they sat and sprawled, how they purred
and preened, how they dabbed and
darted, blinked and batted, skittered
and skulked. He couldn't wait to paint a
picture of Snow. Why hadn't he thought
of it before?

He painted and painted and painted.
Mixed and dotted.
Frowned and
tutted. His first
cat looked like a
polar bear.

The second came out rather like a pig.

The third had something of porcupine
about it.

Vincent just wasn't good at cats.

Perhaps he needed a life-model?

When Skitter next came to his garden –
soon followed by Tabby – he tried to
draw Skitter up in the apple tree, but
she ended up looking like a fruit bat.
After lunch, he took his brushes and
paints along to Jeannie's house, and
asked if Boris would mind posing. Boris
was the ideal model, as he slept all day
long and hardly moved. Vincent
worked all afternoon, but his portrait of
Boris looked like a hippopotamus.

He threw up his hands. "It's no good!
I should have known. I can't paint
people, and I can't paint cats."

"But you *can* paint." Jeannie looked at
the Welsh mountain picture above her
fireplace. "It's just a matter of finding
what to do."

"I don't know."
Vincent was
packing up his
things. "Sometimes
I think I'll never be able
to paint again."

He trailed back to his own house.
What would he do? The art show was
just a month away, and still he had
nothing good enough. He thought of his
half-a-wall at the exhibition, completely
bare. He'd feel so ashamed and useless
that he wouldn't even go to the show,
and then he'd feel even worse.

He found Tom and Tabby at his front
door. They'd just knocked, and were
surprised to see him coming up the
path behind them.

"Oh, there you are!" said Tabby, and handed him a card. "It's an invitation to my birthday party on Saturday. You *will* come, won't you?"

"Thank you, Tabby! I'd like that very much," said Vincent. He felt a little happier as he watched them run back to their own house.

Indoors, just for a moment, he thought he saw a flicker of white, and heard a purr of greeting. He stared and blinked – but no, he must have been mistaken. He propped Tabby's invitation on the mantelpiece, and went to the shed to put away his painting things.

Maybe I should give up trying to paint, he thought to himself. *It only makes me*

unhappy. Why don't I get rid of all this
stuff, and keep gardening tools here instead?
I'm no good any more.

He slid the clumsy cat pictures into
the bottom of a drawer, where he
wouldn't have to look at them.

That night, Vincent dreamed of Snow
again.

Snow was teasing him: nearly
showing himself, then whisking out
of sight.

Vincent followed him through rooms and gardens, down paths and alleyways, trying to catch up. At each corner, each doorway, each turn of a stair, he knew that Snow wasn't far away. But there was nothing to see, not a whisker or a paw print. Snow was too far ahead, just out of sight.

Vincent woke up to his empty room. There was no Snow to come purring in, telling him to get up. No white cat-shape reflected in the mirror. No windowsill-sitter behind the curtain, watching the birds outside.

Snow wasn't there.

I ought to be used to it by now, Vincent thought.

After breakfast, he went out to his

painting shed, without much hope. He turned on his heater. He sat at his easel and looked out at the garden.

A rush of white, a clawing at the bird table – a starling and a pigeon flew off in a great flurry of wings. Vincent caught his breath. *Was it?*

"No, of course not, you silly old fool!"

he told himself,
seeing Skitter's
blue collar as
she balanced on
the bird table.
Bad Skitter!

"Skitty! Skitzy-
cat!" called
Tabby's voice
from the street,
and Skitter
jumped down and ran to her. Vincent
went round the side of the house to call
hello to Tabby. She carried Skitter
indoors, then she and Tom waved to
Vincent as they set off for school.

Once everyone had gone off to school
and work, everything was quiet. It

ought to be good painting time.

Vincent went back to his shed, and sat looking out at the bird table, where Skitter had just perched.

Then he had an idea.

He wasn't good at cats or people, but that didn't mean he couldn't *paint*. Of course he could! What had been stopping him?

His new picture showed a room. It might have looked like a room with no one in it, but somehow it wasn't. The door stood half-open; it was a room that until just now had had a cat in it. There was a vase of flowers on a table, and a hint of purriness; just the trace of a vanishing tail, and a dent in a cushion where a cat had sat. Vincent painted

and painted and painted. When he
stood back to look at his work, he knew
that it was full of life and warmth.

He signed his name, and his heart
swelled with pride.

Chapter Seven

Every day now, Vincent painted, full of new energy. He had a lovely lunch with Jeannie on Thursday, and enjoyed joining in the games at Tabby's birthday party on Saturday, and then he went home and painted some more.

By the weekend of the art show, he'd

finished enough to fill his half-a-wall,
and even to spill out into the corridor.

There was a special party on the
opening night. Jeannie came, and so did
the Pringles. All Vincent's artist friends
were there, too. He admired their
pictures, and they admired his.

"You're on top form, Vincent!
Marvellous!"
"You've been busy!"

"I like this one best. Amazing! Such a
mysterious atmosphere!
How do you do it?"

Vincent smiled, and shook his head modestly. "I don't know. It just turned out like that."

"But, Vincent," said his friend Hamish, peering close. "Have you made a mistake with these labels? All your pictures have got the same title – *The Cat Who Isn't There*. But I don't see a cat in any of them."

Vincent looked at him and raised an eyebrow. Jeannie coughed.

"Oh. Right. I get it," said Hamish. "*The Cat Who Isn't There*. No cat. Very clever."

"But, Hamish," said another friend, Winnie, "you can tell that a cat *was* there just a moment ago, can't you? You can *feel* it."

"Mm. Mmm," went Oscar, peering. "I can almost see my old cat, Freddie."

"And I can see my mum's cat, Daisy," said Justin.

"For me it's the first cat I ever had, years ago – Jim, his name was," said Jeannie.

"I think it's Skitter, gone wandering off again," said Maggie Pringle. "See! She's just this minute gone, and Tabby after her."

"Ahem! Excuse me," said a voice behind them. It was the photographer from the local paper, wanting all the artists to pose in front of the paintings.

In the next *Herald*, there they all are:
smiling, looking proud and modest.
Vincent's in the middle of them,
looking embarrassed.

On the wall behind is a framed
picture marked with a NOT FOR SALE

sticker, the one Vincent's keeping for himself. It's the first of his new paintings, the one that showed him he could still paint. In it there's a room, a vase of flowers, a slightly open door, and a cat who isn't there.

Chapter Eight

After Christmas, Vincent made an important decision.

"I think it's time I looked for another cat," he told Jeannie. "It won't be Snow – I know that. It'll be someone else. But I've waited long enough, now."

Jeannie was delighted. So were Tom and Tabby.

"You must go to the RSPCA!" Tabby told Vincent. "They'll have a cat waiting for you to choose it."

Maggie drove Vincent and the children to the RSPCA animal shelter where Skitter had come from. It made Vincent sad to see so many animals needing homes, and Tabby wished she could have them all.

It was Maggie's idea that Vincent should think about having *two* cats, and no sooner had she said it than two cats in the very next cage caught his eye.

Two black cats, with fur of the blackest black, and eyes of the greenest green. Both had white bibs, and white front paws, as if dipped in milk. They sat very upright, side by side, looking

straight at Vincent. They seemed to
have been waiting for him.

"*Oh!*" went Vincent, and he stopped
by their cage and went no farther.

"Lovely, aren't they?" said the RSPCA
person. "They're a brother and sister."

"They'll need names!" Tabby told
Vincent. "What will you call them?"

But first there were questions to be asked, and forms to be filled in, because everything had to be done properly.

Next day, the RSPCA person came to Vincent's house, to do a home check. Everything was fine.

"Those two cats should think themselves very lucky that you chose them," he told him.

Vincent laughed. "I don't think I chose them, exactly. I think *they* chose *me*."

Now Coal and Soot live happily with Vincent. They've settled in. They know their way around. They've met Skitter and Boris, and although there were a few hissings and swipings at first, they all get on well now.

Soot, or Coal, or both, are often to be found in

the chair in Vincent's hut while he
works. He paints and paints until Tabby
and Tom come to say hello after school,
or until Jeannie comes round for tea and
cake and a chat.

Now, if you were to ask Vincent if he's happy, he'd say, "YES! I most definitely am!"

He hasn't forgotten Snow, of course. Often he thinks of Snow, and dreams of Snow, and – especially when Skitter comes into his garden – thinks for a moment that he *sees* Snow. And he knows that Snow hasn't left him. Not really.

About the author

Linda Newbery loves to write. She also loves her four cats: Holly, Hazel, Finn and Fleur who keep her busy and who have inspired Cat Tales. Linda had her first novel published in 1988 and she's the author of many books for young readers. She has won the Silver Medal Nestlé Children's Book Prize and the Costa Children's Book Award.

Linda writes in a hut in her garden, usually with a cat or two for company.

Cat Tales

Curl up with Cat Tales from award-winning and enchanting storyteller, Linda Newbery.

The Cat with Two Names

Two of everything sounds perfect, but it soon leads to double the trouble for Cat...

ISBN 9780746096147

Rain Cat

Nobody believes that the mysterious cat can control the weather...until it starts to rain!

ISBN 9780746097281

Smoke Cat

Where do the shadowy cats in next door's garden come from and why won't one particular cat join them?

ISBN 9780746097298

Shop Cat

Strange things have started happening in the toy shop since Twister came to stay...

ISBN 9780746097304

The Cat who Wasn't There

Vincent is so lonely without his cat, Snow... until a slim white cat appears in his garden.

ISBN 9780746097328

Ice Cat

Tom's cat is made of snow and ice, so of course it can't come alive...or can it?

ISBN 9780746097311

Amy Wild, Animal Talker

by Diana Kimpton

Collect all of Amy's fun and fur-filled adventures!

The Secret Necklace

Amy doesn't want to move away from her friends to live on Clamerkin Island. But then her great-aunt gives her a secret present — a magical necklace that gives her the power to talk to animals.

ISBN 9781409504290

The Musical Mouse

Amy's first day at her new school is made even more exciting by the appearance of a musical mouse! But Amy's teachers are not so happy about the squeaky visitor...

ISBN 9781409504306

Coming soon...

The Mystery Cat

Amy finds a cat who's lost his memory
and promises to track down his owners.
But she's in for a surprise!

ISBN 9781409504313

The Furry Detectives

Things have been going missing on the
Island and Amy suspects there's an
animal thief at work...

ISBN 9781409504320

For more fun and furry
animal stories, log on to
www.fiction.usborne.com